CW00547741

Loved
by the
Dragon

(Stonefire Dragons #6)

Jessie Donovan

This book is a work of fiction. Names, characters, places, and incidents are either the product of the writer's imagination or are used fictitiously, and any resemblance to actual persons, living or dead, business establishments, events, or locales is entirely coincidental.

Loved by the Dragon
Copyright © 2015 Laura Hoak-Kagey
Mythical Lake Press, LLC
First Paperback Edition

All rights reserved. This book or any portion thereof may not be reproduced or used in any manner without the express written permission of the author except for the use of brief quotations in a book review.

Cover Art by Clarissa Yeo of Yocla Designs.

ISBN 13: 978-1942211334

To Craig Bartz

A great man who was well loved and will live on in many memories

Other Books by Jessie Donovan

Stonefire Dragons
Sacrificed to the Dragon
Seducing the Dragon
Revealing the Dragons
Healed by the Dragon
Reawakening the Dragon
Loved by the Dragon
Surrendering to the Dragon
Cured by the Dragon

Lochguard Highland Dragons
The Dragon's Dilemma
The Dragon Guardian
The Dragon's Heart
The Dragon Warrior (Feb 2017)

Asylums for Magical Threats
Blaze of Secrets
Frozen Desires
Shadow of Temptation
Flare of Promise

Cascade Shifters
Convincing the Cougar
Reclaiming the Wolf
Cougar's First Christmas
Resisting the Cougar

CHAPTER ONE

Evie Marshall changed her position in the bed for the hundredth time in the last hour. While she'd had eight-and-a-half months to come to terms with her swollen body and overabundance of hormones, she usually had Bram's warm, comforting presence at her back.

But not tonight.

Over the past few weeks, Bram had been spending a lot of time with Kai Sutherland, Stonefire's head Protector, and Finn Stewart, the clan leader of the Scottish dragon-shifters. The trio was working on plans to track down the dragon hunters with the help of a human soldier named Rafe Hartley. The rational side of Evie's brain knew protecting the clan was a top priority and that Bram wanted nothing more than to be curled up at her back. Yet her pregnancy made her rational side sit in the time-out corner three-quarters of the time so it could make a fuss.

All she knew was every fiber of her being ached for Bram's touch.

Tears prickled her eyes and Evie brushed them away as she cursed her bloody pregnancy hormones. Whoever said they loved being pregnant had to be lying. Throwing up, gaining weight, and losing control of her true self was the worst experience of her life. And considering she'd been kidnapped and held prisoner for several days by a group of dragon hunters, that was saying something.

Then her baby kicked and Evie placed a hand on her stomach. *Sorry, little one. Mummy loves you, truly. But if you could make your exit sooner rather than later, it would be much appreciated.*

Her baby kicked again. Given their child's stubborn father, the little one was probably not saying yes. It was more likely he or she wanted to hang out in the little swimming pool inside her body for as long as possible.

With a sigh, Evie rolled over and glanced at the glowing white numbers of the bedside clock. Three minutes had passed since the last time she'd checked it. Maybe if she counted dragons flying overhead, she could settle long enough to fall asleep.

Just as she reached three-hundred-and-forty-two, she heard the front door to hers and Bram's cottage slowly creak open. Taking hold of the cricket bat next to the bed, Evie scooted off the mattress and moved to stand to the side of the bedroom door. It could be Bram, but given all of the attacks and danger during her months on Clan Stonefire, Evie wasn't taking any chances.

Someone ascended the stairs and stopped in the hallway. Since Evie was only human and didn't possess keen dragon-shifter eyesight, she could only make out a large, tall shape in the darkness. Tightening her grip on the cricket bat, she waited to see if the intruder would speak.

A familiar teasing voice filled the air. "Since you have the bat at the ready, should I protect my cock, love? I don't recall doing anything to upset you, but I could be wrong and want to be prepared."

Evie sighed and flipped on the light. After blinking a few times, she made out Bram's dark hair, blue eyes, and tall, muscled form in the hallway. "Maybe I should give you a taste of what I'm going to endure in a few weeks' time, if your 'wee Evie,' ever decides to come out at all."

Concern flashed in Bram's eyes and he crossed the space between them. After plucking the bat from her hands and tossing it aside, he engulfed her body in his strong arms. "Are you hurting? Do I need to call Dr. Sid?"

Evie pushed back until she could meet Bram's eyes. She frowned. "For the millionth time, if I need a doctor, I'll let you know." She tilted her head and studied his eyes. "The bigger question right now is why are you back so early? I expected you to be out all night again."

"Finn was irritating the hell out of me, so I hung up on his video conference call."

Evie tried not to smile. "One day you will admit he's like the brother you never had."

Bram growled. "If he'd truly been my brother, I would've killed him as a teenager. Be glad that he isn't, because then I would be serving a life sentence in prison and wouldn't be able to do this."

Bram nuzzled her and lightly nipped where her neck met her shoulder. As he licked the light sting, Evie leaned into his touch. "At some point, that is going to stop working on me."

His breath was hot against her skin when he murmured, "If that ever happens, love, then drive a stake through my heart because my life wouldn't be worth living."

Her heart thumped harder and tears prickled her eyes again. "Bram."

He leaned back and his pupils flashed to slits and back. "You know my dragon doesn't like you crying, love."

Evie sniffed. "Tell your dragon it's his fault then for impregnating me. I hope little Murray and the new baby are enough to complete our family because I don't think I can do this again. I can't help the clan or try to locate my missing friend,

Alice, when the merest action turns me into a blubbery mess. As it is, it takes all of the energy I have not to break down in public."

~ ~ ~

Bram Moore-Llewellyn caressed his mate's cheek. "I'm not sure if two babies are enough."

Evie blinked. "What?"

His dragon growled. *Don't provoke her. It's not good for the baby. Evie crying and feeling sad isn't good for the babe. I have a plan.*

His beast merely shook his head and waited to see what Bram would do.

Bram answered, "Two isn't enough. We should have three, maybe four."

Evie narrowed her eyes. "You find a way to carry a child for nine months and birth them, and then we'll talk about it. Until you do, it's not going to happen."

The corner of his mouth ticked up at her growly voice. "I'm sure I have ways of convincing you."

Evie looked around. "Where's that bat?"

"After all, there are a lot of half-dragon-shifter babies in the world who are looking for parents."

His mate met his eyes again. "Are you talking about adoption?" He nodded and she lightly slapped her chest. "Then why the bloody hell didn't you say that from the beginning?"

Grinning, he pulled Evie close. "Because I love how your cheeks turn pink when you're angry and determined to change my mind about something."

"Bram Moore-Llewellyn, I am eight-and-a-half-months pregnant and chock-full of hormones. Under normal circumstances, I would be able to restrain myself from killing you. But right now, it's starting to look like the better option."

Bram winked. "You know you love me." She growled in response, and he leaned down to her ear to whisper, "Besides, you're no longer about to cry. You really should be thanking me, love. I know how you hate to cry."

As he kissed her cheek, Evie let out a sigh. "Sometimes, I wish you weren't so bloody exhausting."

"Then you'd be bored." Brushing her cheek with his own, he murmured, "I'm sorry I've been away so much lately."

Evie snuggled into his chest. "I will always support you, Bram. You know that."

"I sense a 'but.'"

"But I can't seem to get comfortable and fall asleep without you by my side."

He leaned back and cupped her cheek. As he stroked her soft skin with his thumb, he never broke his gaze. "With enough planning and luck, you'll soon be begging me to leave you alone because I'll be around all the time."

Evie raised a red eyebrow. "You'd better be around because I'm not about to raise a newborn by myself. We've been lucky with Murray. He's a very mellow child. Our unborn son or daughter, however, will probably be a stubborn half-dragon hellion."

He grinned. "Maybe that should be her middle name— Hellion."

Evie smacked his side. "One, we don't know it's a girl. And two, that is the worst middle name of all time."

"Hmm, what about Ninjamaster? I like the sound of that."

Evie rolled her eyes. "Why I ever agreed to let you pick the middle name is beyond me."

13

"You won the right to choose the first name, and I needed something."

His mate leaned against his chest again. "We'll see if I veto your choice or not, Bram. We'll see."

As Evie melted further against him, Bram's dragon spoke up. *I don't like the circles under her eyes. Stop teasing her and take her to bed. Soon we won't be able to fuck her for months. I want her tonight. It will help her relax and fall asleep.*

Sex is the last thing on her mind, dragon. Stop asking.

It might help induce labor. Suggest that and Evie will be riding us before you can blink twice.

Bram sighed and Evie asked, "I saw your pupils flashing. What does your dragon want now?" He debated how much to tell her, but Evie continued, "Over the last few weeks, the only time you hesitate is when your beast brings up sex. He really is akin to a randy teenager, isn't he?"

Bram chuckled. "Aye, I won't deny it. Although he made a fair point about sex maybe inducing labor."

Evie pulled back, her eyes bright. *Bloody hell.* That meant she had a plan.

His mate poked his chest. "Brilliant, Bram. None of the teas have worked on their own, nor have the long walks I've been taking, but a little rough dragon sex might just do the trick."

He blinked. "Pardon?"

Evie pulled away, gripped his hand, and tugged. "You're going to try to induce labor." She tugged again. "Come on."

He slowly followed her. "You do know how to romance a dragonman, lass. I'll give you that."

Evie looked over her shoulder and her brows drew together. "Don't sound over enthused about it. I know I'm the

14

size of a large ship at this point, but my boobs are bigger. That has to be a plus."

His dragon growled. *She doubts her beauty. I don't like it. Me neither.*

Stopping in his tracks, Bram drew Evie toward him and looped an arm around her waist. With his free hand, he threaded his fingers through her long, red hair. "You are still the most beautiful female I've ever seen, Evie Marie." He moved his hand down to her swollen belly. "The fact you're large with our child makes you even sexier."

Evie looked unconvinced. Bram's dragon snarled. *Try harder or I will take control and show her just how much we want her.*

Ignoring his dragon, Bram leaned down until he was an inch from Evie's lips. "If you're not convinced with my words of how beautiful you are, then I'll just have to show you."

Before Evie could reply, he lifted her and gently laid her on the bed. In the next instant, he was at her side and leaning over her upper body. "You're mine, love, and you always will be."

And he kissed her.

~ ~ ~

A part of Evie hoped sex with Bram would induce labor. Then she could do what she did best and plan. A baby would create a schedule and routine. Pregnancy did nothing but disrupt it.

Yet as Bram's tongue stroked against hers, Evie forgot all about her goal of inducing labor and simply enjoyed the spicy, male taste of her dragonman. He'd kissed her a million times before, but Bram made each time feel as if it were the first all over again by devouring her mouth with his tongue, nipping her lips, and suckling them after.

Threading her fingers through his hair, she dug her nails into his scalp. She could barely remember being tired. She wanted Bram.

She lifted her torso until her nipples grazed his chest. Bram growled and broke their kiss. "I was going to be noble, wrap you in my arms, and let you fall asleep."

"And now?"

He nipped her bottom lip. "Now, I'm not going to be gentle and make love. I'm going to fuck and claim you all over again."

A thrill rushed through her body and ended between her legs. While she enjoyed slow and gentle at times, she wanted what could be her last time having sex for months to be more. Much more.

Evie moved her chest against Bram's. The friction of her nightshirt felt good against her nipples. Evie opened her legs. "Then feel how ready I am for you, Bram."

Bram ran a hand between them to tug her sensitive nipple and Evie moaned. It was only a matter of time before lying on her back would hurt, but she couldn't resist murmuring, "Again."

Rolling her nipple between his thumb and forefinger, Bram leaned down to kiss the spot behind her ear. The light caress combined with his pinching of her nipple sent a rush of wetness between her thighs. "Bram."

He growled. "That's better. I never want to hear sadness in your voice when you say my name."

She opened her mouth to make a retort, but then her dragonman ripped open her nightshirt and took both of her breasts in his palms. As he ran his rough skin back and forth over her tight buds, Evie planted her feet on the bed and opened her legs. "Stop teasing me. I want to feel your hands between my thighs."

Bram's nostrils flared as his pupils flashed to slits. "The second I do, you'll be on your hands and knees with my cock inside of you. My dragon is nearly as impatient as he was right before the mate-claim frenzy finally broke loose."

Rather than ruin the sexy mood by mentioning her back was starting to hurt, because Bram would turn into the overprotective mate she knew all too well, Evie widened her legs further in invitation. "I can take whatever you dish out, dragonman. If you haven't learned that by now, you never will."

With a snarl, Bram took her lips in a rough kiss as his fingers played with her pussy. He teased her opening and Evie cried out. Pulling away, Bram searched her eyes. "Are you all right?"

With a growl, Evie answered, "Ask me that one more time and I swear I'll find someone else to help induce labor."

Knowing her taunt would stoke his dragon, Bram didn't waste time. He lifted and turned her over until she was on her hands and knees. He tore off the remainder of her nightshirt. "You're mine, Evie Marie." He slapped her arse and then plunged his cock into her. "Only mine."

Looking over her shoulder, she raised her brows. "Then show me, dragonman. Claim me as you promised, no holds barred."

Indecision flashed on his face for a second before it was replaced with a set jaw and steely eyes. Good. Bram's stubbornness had won out.

Then her mate gripped her hips and pulled out before slamming back in, hard. He repeated the action and Evie gripped the nearest pillow and rested her head on it. Bram paused and rather than yell at him, she wiggled her hips. That was the only invitation Bram needed before he moved again. Each thrust increased in pace until his balls were slapping against her flesh and Evie closed her eyes to savor each delicious intrusion of his long, hard cock.

~~~

Bram barely had his dragon under control. His bloody mate's taunts and challenges had stirred his beast. It seemed as if his dragon would never learn.

His dragon spoke up. *I know what she does. But it gives us the chance to take advantage and fuck her hard.*

His beast sent a torrent of lust through Bram's body. To appease both man and beast, Bram increased his pace and slapped Evie's arse again.

The action soothed his dragon and Bram could focus back on pleasing his mate. She needed to know that no matter what she looked like, she would always be the most beautiful female in the world to him.

Rubbing Evie's slightly pink bum, he continued moving in and out of her pussy as he roamed down the side of her body and to her breast. He cupped her, loving the heavy weight in his hands.

All too soon he wouldn't be able to enjoy his mate's curves in his hand as he fucked her.

His beast snarled. *Then make it count.*

When his dragon wasn't near the edge as he was in the moment, Bram knew his beast would agree the upcoming months would be some of the happiest of their lives, even without sex. *Bloody dragon. I'm trying.*

Bram gave Evie's breast one gentle squeeze before he roamed down her belly and to her clit. Rubbing in hard, slow circles, Evie finally raised her head again with a cry. "Yes, harder."

Pressing against her swollen bud, he increased his pace with his thumb and his hips. As Evie moaned, he smiled. His mate always did prefer double stimulation. "Are you ready to come for me, love? I want to feel you grip my dick."

In the first few months of their mating, it had taken a lot more torture with his fingers and tongue to get her to come for him. It still always surprised him when she whispered, "You know what I like. Do it, and I'll come."

With a growl, Bram stopped circling her clit and rubbed back and forth, increasing the pressure with each pass. Evie cried out, "Bram," as her pussy clutched his cock as she came. Both man and beast reveled in the hot embrace.

Taking her hips with both hands, Bram let loose his dragon and together they pounded into their mate harder, as if it were the first time. The sound of flesh slapping against flesh filled the room and it increased the pressure at his spine. With a roar, he stilled inside Evie and came hard. Each jet of semen was a new claim on his mate, spinning her into orgasm after orgasm. He would never tire of her cries of pleasure.

When Evie wrung out the last drop from his cock, Bram laid his forehead on her shoulder and rubbed her belly in slow circles. "Did it work or do we need to try again? I'll do it as many times as it takes to help bring about labor."

Evie reached behind her and swatted his thigh. She drawled, "I'm sure that's your main aim."

Hearing the tiredness in her voice, Bram gently wrapped his arms around Evie and lifted until she was sitting on his lap. He kissed her damp neck before murmuring, "Of course. I'm clan leader and I'm always noble. Most especially when it comes to sex."

She snorted and looked over her shoulder. "Sure, and I'm the queen of abstinence."

The corner of his mouth ticked up and he placed a possessive hand over their baby. "Next you're going to tell me this is a result of a turkey baster."

Evie grinned and Bram stopped breathing. She was so bloody beautiful. Yet somehow he focused on her words as she answered, "I haven't used that one yet. I think tomorrow I'll start spreading it around, about how shy you are, so I had to use a turkey baster."

Bram growled and hugged her tighter against him. "Do that and I really will pick Ninjamaster as the wee one's middle name."

Evie smiled and leaned against him. "Then hope the baby comes out soon. If I'm screaming and trying to push your giant dragon child out of my vagina, I won't have a chance to spread the turkey baster rumor."

He laid his chin on her shoulder. "I don't want you to be in pain ever, Evie." He held her even closer. "As it is, I might lose you."

Evie shook her head. "Nonsense, Bram. We're having only one child, I'm your true mate, *and* I'm healthy."

His dragon huffed. *Don't upset her. She won't die.*

But you don't know that. Look what happened to Melanie and she was both a true mate and healthy when she birthed the twins. Even so, her heart stopped beating for about thirty seconds.

Evie's stubbornness alone will win out. You'll see.

As Bram and Evie fell into a comfortable silence, Bram secretly hoped so. He'd had his true mate and best friend for less than a year. More than that, Murray needed his mum.

Kissing Evie's cheek, Bram decided he would stop worrying and focus on lending Evie his strength. When the time came, she might just need it.

CHAPTER TWO

Snapped out of her peaceful slumber with a sharp pain in her abdomen, Evie just barely managed to not cry out. She'd had a few Braxton Hicks contractions over the last week and the last thing she needed was for Bram to bang on Sid's door and wake the dragonwoman doctor up when it was unnecessary.

Taking a deep breath, she rubbed her belly with one hand and waited.

After thirty seconds, the pain passed and she released her breath. Glancing to the clock, she noted the time.

Evie moved slowly to the edge of the bed, but before she could put her feet on the floor, Bram's sleepy voice filled the room. "Is everything okay, Evie?"

"Can't I go to the bathroom without you worrying?"

Bram reached over and patted her thigh. "No."

With a sigh, she squeezed Bram's hand. "Once I know I'm really in labor, I'll let you know."

"Then what was that sharp intake of breath a minute ago?"

Bloody dragonman and his super senses. "I already experienced a fake labor earlier this week. The second I know it's for real, believe me, I'll be asking for all the help I can get."

Bram's voice was gravelly as he answered, "Good. Now hurry up and use the toilet so you can come back to me and I can keep tabs on you."

Too tired to argue, Evie merely shook her head and released Bram's hand. "Fine. May I go now?"

Bram released his hold. "I'm giving you five minutes and then I'm coming after you."

Hefting herself off the bed, Evie muttered, "Overprotective dragonman," and rushed into the bathroom. She flipped the light on and blinked for her eyes to adjust to the brightness. If the painful contraction, real or otherwise, wasn't enough, a headache throbbed right behind her eyes.

Placing a hand on either side of the counter, she glared at her protruding belly. *This is it, baby. You'd better be trying to come out for real.*

Silence was her answer.

Evie did her business and washed her hands. Her fingers were even more swollen than earlier in the day. They may as well have been sausages.

Looking up at the mirror, her puffy face greeted her. In fact, it was puffier than before Bram had come home. Evie frowned at her reflection. She teased Bram for being overprotective, but between the puffiness, sudden headache, and the pain in her abdomen, Evie's gut told her something was off. As much as she hated to do it, she was going to have to worry Bram.

As if on cue, Bram knocked on the bathroom door and opened it. His gaze moved to where she was standing at the counter. In the next second, he walked over to stand next to her. Caressing her forehead, he asked, "What's wrong? And don't try to brush it off this time, Evie Marie. I see it in your eyes."

Her heart thudded in her chest. "I don't know, Bram. It may be nothing, but between the swelling and sudden headache, something seems off. I think you should call Dr. Sid."

Bram nodded and rushed into the bedroom for his mobile phone. Evie started to follow him, but another pain rippled across her belly and she cried out. She'd barely had time to lean against the wall for support when Bram had his hands on her shoulders. She heard the dominance in his voice as he growled out, "We're going to call Dr. Sid the second this pain passes and tell her to come over."

Evie breathed through the contraction. The second it stopped, she took a deep breath and murmured, "You won't get any complaints from me."

Bram's pupils flashed to slits and back. "I hear the pain in your voice, love." He rubbed her lower back and supported her to the bed. He nodded toward the mattress. "Lay down while I call the doctor."

With a pounding head, she slowly lowered herself onto the bed, turned onto her side, and hugged her stomach. If this was the beginning of labor, then Evie started to wonder if wishing for it had been the best thing after all.

~ ~ ~

Five minutes later, Bram ran a hand through his hair while Evie clutched his other hand and screamed. Sid was on her way, but every time Evie cried out, his fear of losing her only increased.

His beast snarled and spoke up. *We won't lose her. She is our true mate. She will live.*

It's not guaranteed. Dragon-shifter hormones can kill a human in labor, and you know it.

Shoving his beast aside, he focused on Evie. When her shouts died down, he squeezed her hand and brushed back a few strands of hair from her damp forehead. "It looks like you got your wish, Evie Marie. I think you're in real labor."

"And you're a doctor now?"

The corner of his mouth ticked up. "Maybe. I'm always on the lookout to expand my skills."

Evie shook her head. "I'm too tired to argue. You're not a doctor, end of story. I'll take my medical advice from Sid."

Bram cupped Evie's cheek. "I suppose I can live with that."

"Bram."

He didn't like the worry in her voice. "Don't even think about saying you could be dying. You won't die. I won't let you."

A knock on the front door caused his dragon to shout. *Answer it. Evie needs relief.*

Bram debated leaving his mate alone, but Evie rolled her eyes and said, "Go answer the door. Nothing is going to happen to me in the sixty seconds you're away."

"Promise? If you give me your word, then I trust your stubbornness to see it through."

She snorted. "Not sure if that's exactly true, but I promise."

"Good." Bram slowly released her hand and stood up. "I'll be right back."

Evie muttered some choice words about caveman dragon-shifters, but Bram ignored them as he raced down the stairs and opened the front door. Dr. Cassidy Jackson, better known as Dr. Sid, stood in the doorway with a medical bag in her hand. She made a shooing motion with her free hand. "Yes, I'll help her. And no, I can't perform miracles. Just get out of the way, Bram."

With anyone else, he would frown and maybe growl. However, Sid was one of the few he trusted with not only his life but also the lives of his clan members. Stepping aside, Sid rushed past. Bram followed. "Evie's had another possible contraction. Her screams are killing me, Sid. Find a way to help her."

Sid tossed over her shoulder. "I'm not a human doctor, but I'll see what I can do until help arrives."

"Help? What help? You didn't clear it with me earlier."

"I don't have to, as you bloody well know. Medical issues are completely left up to me. Besides, I asked a favor of your best friend up in Scotland. Help should be coming."

Bram growled. "Finlay Stewart isn't my best friend. What did you ask for?"

"They have a human woman there named Holly MacKenzie. She used to be a midwife with the NHS before mating one of the Scottish dragon-shifters. Her mate and a few of Clan Lochguard's Protectors are flying her down so she can help me with Evie."

Bram had heard of the details from both Melanie Hall-MacLeod and Finn about the human sacrifice. "Holly MacKenzie had better know what the bloody hell she's doing."

Sid met his eyes for a second and raised her brows before turning back around and walking into Bram and Evie's room.

Knowing Sid, that was all the answer he was going to get.

His dragon spoke up. *Sid has never steered us wrong before. Besides, she has authority over even you when it comes to medical issues in Stonefire.*

Now Finn will lord it over me the next time we talk.

Does it matter if it helps our mate?

His beast's words put everything into perspective. *You're far calmer than me in all of this.*

Someone has to be. Besides, I would do anything for Evie.

27

His dragon fell quiet. Bram kneeled on the opposite side of the bed from Sid and took Evie's hand. His mate smiled at him and whether she knew it or not, the action gave him strength.

Content to stare into his mate's eyes and hold her hand, the pair of them remained silent until Sid finished her preliminary examination. Sid placed her hands on her hips. "It's possible you're in labor, Evie, although we need to wait a little longer since your water hasn't broken yet. But I'm a little concerned about the swelling. Bram also mentioned over the phone that a headache came on suddenly. Is there anything else I should know?"

Evie answered, "My vision has also started to blur a bit, but it could just be because I'm tired."

Sid nodded. "Possibly. Or, it could be preeclampsia. Since dragon-shifter females don't get preeclampsia, I'll wait for Holly's opinion before starting any treatments."

Bram frowned. "Treatments? Just what the bloody hell is preeclampsia?"

Sid's expression remained neutral, irritating Bram further. Just how the hell could she remain so calm?

Sid replied, "Something we can manage if caught in time. I just need to watch Evie's blood pressure and check her urine. If it turns out Evie has it, I'll give her some magnesium sulfate."

Bram growled, but Evie squeezed his hand and he met his mate's eyes. "Yelling at Sid isn't going to help anything. It might even push my blood pressure higher. Right now, I need your strength, Bram. Will you lend it to me?"

His expression relaxed and he kissed the back of Evie's hand. "Anything for you, love. Anything at all. Just ask."

Evie's face relaxed a fraction. "Then lay next to me and hold me in your arms. Your touch always helps to erase my stress."

Bram looked to Sid and the dragonwoman nodded. "Evie needs a little rest. Later, you might need to help her walk around the room to help speed up the process." Sid picked up her medical bag. "I'll be back as soon as I can. Holly should be here before much longer and I want to fill her in on everything. If you two need anything, I have my mobile phone in my pocket. I'll also send along a nurse to keep watch and test Evie's urine for proteins."

Evie murmured, "Thanks, Sid," and the doctor exited the room.

Lying next to Evie's back, Bram engulfed his mate in his arms and breathed in her scent. "We don't know when another contraction will come, love, so doze as much as you can. I'll watch over you."

"I love you, Bram."

"I love you, too, Evie Marie."

Evie snuggled her arse against his groin and Bram tightened his grip on his female. As she relaxed against him, Bram closed his eyes and reveled in the heat and softness of his mate.

His dragon paced in the back of his mind and Bram couldn't bring himself to tell his beast to stop. In a way, it helped relieve his own nervous energy. Sid couldn't come back soon enough with Holly MacKenzie.

CHAPTER THREE

Evie was sorely tempted to cut off Bram's balls so that she'd never be pregnant again.

Another contraction had just finished and she was still trying to catch her breath.

Bram wiped her brow and she glared up at him. "I am never doing this again, Bram. Never. You're getting a vasectomy as soon as the baby is out."

Bram removed the cloth from her forehead and shook his head. "It's just the labor talking. After you finally hold our wee Evie and gaze at her soft, pink face, then you'll forget all about the pain."

"Forget about the pain, my arse. How about we push a grape up your penis and then we'll talk."

Bram shifted his legs. Good. He deserved some sympathy discomfort. "If I could take the pain away from you, love, I would. But I can't. So if thinking up ways to abuse my cock and balls helps in anyway, go right ahead. None of them will come true, though."

The nurse sent to watch over Evie was currently downstairs doing some kind of test on her urine, so Evie didn't have long to make her dreams a reality. She looked around the room to see if she could use anything to show Bram how wrong he was when Sid walked through the door with a dark-haired woman. Right behind the dark-haired woman was one of the MacKenzie twins; Evie would recognize the auburn hair, tall build, and blue eyes anywhere. Because of the scar near his left eye, she knew it was the younger twin, Fraser.

Without preamble, Sid motioned to the woman. "This is Holly MacKenzie. Holly, meet Evie Marshall."

Evie had heard of the human woman before, but due to her advanced pregnancy, hadn't made it up to Lochguard to meet her. "Hello, Holly. I would offer you a cup of tea and some biscuits, but I'd probably drop the lot as soon as my next contraction hits."

Holly smiled. "My mother-in-law feeds me so many biscuits and scones that I'd pop if I ate any more. Thanks, anyway."

Evie grinned. "Lorna MacKenzie does like to bake. I keep telling Bram to invite all of Finn's family down here so Aunt Lorna could teach me something. I have a tendency to burn toast, so there's a lot of room for improvement."

Bram grunted, but it was Sid who spoke up. "Enough with the pleasantries. Bram, Fraser, I want you out of the room for five or ten minutes so that Holly and I can exam Evie properly without either one of you hovering over my shoulder."

Evie's dragonman growled. "No bloody way I'm leaving Evie."

Sid crossed her arms over her chest. "Go or I will inject you with a sleeping drug and Fraser can drag your arse down the stairs. I might even hint for him to tie you up so you can't escape. I need Evie as calm as possible and that won't happen with you growling every two seconds. Especially with what I might need to do if we think she has preeclampsia. So, which will it be?"

Fraser rubbed his hands together. "I vote for the second."

Holly slapped Fraser's side. "Stop it."

Fraser shrugged and Evie couldn't help but smile. Holly had sacrificed herself to the Scottish dragon clan to help her father, but it looked like Holly had fallen in love with a dragonman in the process.

Evie hoped one day it would always be that way with the human sacrifices.

When all Bram did was stare at Sid, Evie sighed. "You can run up the stairs in about three seconds if anything happens. Hell, you can even post guards outside if it'll help ease your nerves. But if Sid needs to see me, then let her do it. She probably has drugs and I very much want them."

Holly spoke up. "Actually, research has shown that pain medication and anesthesia usually elevates dragon-shifter hormone levels and increases the risk of death. You're going to have to do this au natural."

Evie blinked. "What? No drugs?"

Holly answered, "Not the pain-killing kind. I'm sure Dr. Sid has mentioned it before, although you are a little early, so maybe she was saving it. Regardless, the research is sound, so we're going to follow it."

For a human, Holly MacKenzie sure knew how to thread her voice with dominance. It had to be her midwifery training.

Sid took a pre-filled needle from her medical bag and held it up. "I don't make idle threats. Out, Bram, or you're going to be taking a long nap."

Fraser fist-pumped the air and Bram narrowed his eyes. "Fine, I'll go. I won't give Finn's bloody cousin the satisfaction of dragging me around. Finn would never let me live it down." He looked to Evie. "Call my name if you need anything, Evie. I'll come running." He cupped her cheek. "And don't be stubborn and wait until the last possible moment to ask for my help. We're going to do this together."

Evie placed her hand over Bram's. "Of course I'll ask for help. Believe me, I will be shouting your name seven ways to Sunday once the baby comes. And not all in loving tones, I might add."

Bram grinned. "I can handle that." He gave her a gentle kiss and moved toward the door. "Take care of her, Sid. She has my heart and I can't bear to lose it."

Tears filled Evie's eyes, but she managed to hold them back. Bram would never leave if she started crying.

Sid nodded. "I will do everything I can."

With that, Bram exited the room. Fraser kissed Holly deeply, Evie was pretty sure it involved a lot of tongue, and then also left the room.

Holly was the first to speak. "Right, then. I'm going to check your blood pressure again. The protein levels in your urine were high, so you're at risk for preeclampsia. We're going to have to keep a close eye on you."

Evie's stomach dropped a little and she placed a hand over her belly. "Should I be worried?"

Sid spoke up. "At the moment, everything is manageable. Truth be told, I'm more worried about elevated dragon-shifter hormones. As soon as Holly's done checking your BP, we'll draw some more blood."

Evie raised her brows. "What if both my blood pressure and dragon hormone levels are high? What happens then?"

Sid answered, "Then we start administering drugs that won't interact with the dragon-shifter hormones in your body." She waved at Holly. "Holly is up on the latest research and together we can decide the best course of treatment."

Evie looked from Sid to Holly and back again. "That's a lot of medical speak that tells me absolutely nothing. You've always been straightforward with me, Sid. Don't start beating around the bush now."

Sid raised an eyebrow. "If you have both preeclampsia and elevated dragon hormones, your chances of dying in childbirth increases 10 percent. That gives you a 40 percent chance of surviving. I hate asking you to keep it from Bram, but it might be best. His overprotectiveness will cause you stress. That's why I sent him downstairs."

Rubbing her belly, Evie nodded solemnly. "That's all I wanted to know and I understand about Bram. He's already convinced I'm going to die."

Holly squeezed Evie's shoulder. "But we don't know if you're at higher risk yet. Let's do the exam, take some blood, and I'll help you to the toilet to collect another urine sample."

Not wanting to think about what could go wrong or how she could die soon, Evie jumped on the chance of a distraction. "I wasn't expecting to need help to the toilet until I was old and wrinkly. I guess I should get used to a lack of modesty from here on out."

Holly grinned. "Having a bairn means tossing modesty to the wind. Better accept that now. Although you've been mated to a dragon-shifter for nearly a year, so I would think you'd be used to their casual nature about nudity."

Evie raised her brows. "Would your mate allow you to parade around naked?"

"He'd probably try to kill anyone who saw me."

Evie nodded. "Exactly. Imagine a mate even more protective than yours, and that's Bram. All hell would break loose."

Holly opened her mouth, but another contraction rolled across her abdomen. Evie closed her eyes and drew in a breath.

Holly murmured breathing instructions and Evie forgot about everything else but trying to follow them.

~~~

Bram paced the living room, clenching and unclenching his fingers as he went. How could Sid kick him out of the room? Bram had studied the delivery process both with Evie and on his own. He might not be a doctor, but his mate would need him when the time came.

His beast spoke up. *It's not as if Evie is going to drop a baby in the next five minutes. Let Sid examine her and ensure our mate is okay. If there's something wrong, then Sid needs time to try and fix it.*

Just because you're right doesn't mean I have to agree with you.

Before his dragon could reply, Fraser MacKenzie's voice filled the room. "Wearing a hole in the floor won't help her, Bram. I tried that myself last month, and the only thing that helped my female was to take action when it was needed."

Bram glanced over at the tall, auburn-haired Scot. "I heard about your reckless rescue attempt. But answer me this—when you knew your mate could be hurting, did you calmly sit by and go about your business?"

"Of course not. But I'm not a clan leader. You are. Expectations are higher for you."

He turned toward Fraser. "Finn might let you talk to him that way, but I'm not your cousin. Be careful, Fraser MacKenzie, or I'll toss you off my land."

The bastard grinned. "Finn thought you might say that. And he said that if you ever want to step foot on Lochguard to see Arabella's babies, then you'd better be nice to me. That includes not kicking me off your land, I might add."

Arabella was originally from Clan Stonefire and was the closest thing Bram had to a little sister. "I am going to kill Finlay Stewart one of these days."

Fraser shrugged. "You can try."

Bram walked up to the Scottish dragonman and narrowed his eyes. "Now is not the time to test me, lad. I earned the right to be clan leader with blood and sweat. You wouldn't be much of a challenge."

Someone pounding on the front door prevented Fraser from answering. After glaring another two seconds at Fraser for good measure, Bram went to answer the door. His dragon sniffed. *Someone's looking for a fight.*

I know how to knock a male flat on his arse; it's a tangible enemy. It gives me something to think about since I can't fight any sort of pregnancy complications Evie might face.

Try to be a little more positive. She is strong and stubborn. If she can handle us, she can handle anything.

Bram ignored his dragon and opened the door to find Tristan and Melanie standing in the doorway. A quick peek told him they hadn't brought their twins. "What the bloody hell are you two doing here?"

Melanie poked him in the chest. "One of my dearest friends is about to have a baby. At least Sid thought to send me a text message."

Bram looked to Tristan and his friend shrugged one shoulder. "Mel wanted to come."

Since Tristan would do most anything for his mate, Bram looked back to Melanie. "You can come in, but only if you keep the Scottish bastard out of my hair."

37

As if on cue, Fraser appeared at Bram's side with a grin. Looking to Melanie, he bowed. "My lady."

Tristan grunted and Melanie laughed before replying, "I've heard a lot about you from Arabella. It's nice to meet you in person."

Fraser winked. "Likewise. It's not every day you meet the famous human who changed some of the laws for dragon-shifters."

Melanie sighed. "A little. But there's still a long way to go."

Tristan wrapped an arm around Melanie's waist and pulled her close. With a scowl, he demanded, "Which twin are you?"

Fraser studied Tristan a second and then answered, "I'm Fraser. And what Arabella's told me so far hasn't done you justice."

Tristan hugged Melanie closer. "And what the bloody hell has my sister been saying?"

Shrugging, Fraser answered, "Oh, not much. Just that she used you as an example when describing the exact opposite of my family."

Melanie beat Tristan to the reply. "That's why we should've gone to visit again, Tristan. Whether you like it or not, Finn is the father of your nieces or nephews. You need to show him the lovely man you've become, especially since the last time you saw him, you all but challenged him to a fight."

Bram growled and stepped between everyone. "On second thought, Mel and Tristan, take Fraser out of my cottage and keep him preoccupied. I can't take much more of this."

Fraser's grin faded and something fierce flashed in the dragonman's blue eyes. "I'm not leaving my mate alone. It's dangerous enough that Holly left Lochguard at all. I won't risk someone trying to take her from me again."

Bram's respect for Fraser raised a notch. "Nothing will happen to her whilst I'm here, I promise. She is a guest and if she helps Evie, I will be in her debt."

Fraser crossed his arms over his chest. "If I leave, so does Holly."

Mel interjected, "Just let him stay. Fraser can help me make some tea." She looked up at Tristan. "You can release me at any time, Tristan." Her mate grunted and she merely waited.

With a sigh, Tristan released his mate. "Fine. But if he so much as touches you, I will kick his arse."

Fraser opened his mouth to reply, but Bram stepped between the two. "Enough. Tristan, I need to talk to you alone. Let Mel make some tea. Fraser isn't about to betray his true mate. His dragon won't let him."

Just as Tristan muttered, "Fine," Melanie walked up to Fraser and motioned toward the kitchen. "Come with me, Fraser. I want to hear all about your mating ceremony. Holly mentioned a few details, but I want to hear it from your side of things. After that, you can help me watch baby Murray."

Fraser's jaw unclenched. "I'm sure I can't top what my lass already told you, but I can never tell that story enough. The room was decorated with silver fabric…"

Mel winked at Bram. "We'll be back soon. Then Tristan, Fraser and I can watch Murray while you focus on Evie."

Bram didn't want to admit it, but Melanie was right. As much as he didn't trust Fraser, Melanie and Tristan would protect wee Murray with their lives.

He nodded. Mel and Fraser left the room.

The second they were alone, Bram let his collected exterior down. "Tristan, how did you do it? Evie's nowhere near birthing our child and both my nerves *and* dragon are frazzled."

Tristan remained quiet for a second before replying, "She'll need you and you do what you can."

Bram raised an eyebrow. "You can pretend to be a distant arsehole with everyone else, but it won't work with me, Tristan. Stop pretending and just tell me the truth. I'm your oldest friend. I deserve that much."

"Honestly? You're going to feel as if someone is ripping out your heart. The few seconds Melanie's heart stopped beating were the longest and worst of my life. But I never gave up hope. Because the second you do, she'll feel it and might give it up as well."

Bram clapped his friend's shoulder. "Then I won't let Evie down." He motioned with his head toward the living room. "I don't usually drink alcohol, but I think I need some right about now."

As they walked into the living room, Bram took comfort from Tristan's presence. If Tristan and Melanie could survive birthing two babies, then Evie would be fine with one. Even if he had to perform CPR himself, he wouldn't allow Evie to die.

His dragon spoke up. *I'm glad you finally agree with what I've been saying the whole time.*

Sometimes, dragon, a person needs to hear it from a second source as well.

His beast huffed. *If you merely listen to me next time from the start, then it will save time. Remember that.*

As his dragon retreated to the back of his mind, Bram took out a bottle of whiskey and poured two glasses. Just as he clinked glasses with Tristan, Evie screamed. Every iota of his being urged him to rush upstairs, but he didn't want to interrupt Sid and Holly, or he'd face Sid's wrath.

Tossing back his drink, Bram hated the fact he wasn't able to control the situation.

Chapter Four

Sixteen hours later, Evie's upper body was strapped to a hospital bed in Sid's surgery and Bram wasn't sure how much longer he could handle his beautiful mate contained and in so much pain.

Labor was bad enough, but Dr. Sid had put Evie on a magnesium sulfate IV drip several hours ago and ever since, his mate had trouble focusing and complained of feeling as if she was floating slightly out of her body.

Except for when a contraction hit. Then every straining muscle and stab of pain brought her screaming back.

Bram wiped her forehead with a damp cloth and murmured, "You're nearly there, love."

When all Evie did was sigh, Bram's heart squeezed. What he wouldn't give for her to have the strength to argue with him. If only he could do something—anything—to help ease his mate's discomfort.

Sid's authoritative voice filled the room. "The induction medication has nearly done its job, Evie. Let's get the baby out so we can get your blood pressure back under control."

Bram growled. "You need to work on your bedside manner, Sid."

All Evie could do was squeeze Bram's hand in hers. "No, I prefer the truth."

Bram's face softened and he kissed her forehead. "I just want you out of those straps and back in my arms, love."

Sid jumped in. "And she will be once the baby is out and Evie's vitals are within normal levels again."

Bram ignored the doctor and focused on his mate. His dragon spoke up. *I think the baby is ready to come out.*

How do you know? You're not a bloody psychic.

I sense our baby's dragon. It's impatient.

Even though a dragon-shifter's dragon half couldn't communicate with them until six or seven years old, even a baby sensed their other half lurking in the back of his or her mind. Dragons couldn't talk with one another, but sometimes they did sense each other's moods. *To be honest, I'm impatient too.*

Evie clenched his hand tightly and he focused back on his mate as she whispered, "Another one is coming."

Holly moved next to the vitals monitor. "Her blood pressure is stable but not going down, Dr. Sid. Please tell me she's fully dilated."

Sid glanced at the monitor. A second later, she moved back between Evie's legs and then looked up. "Evie, you're fully dilated. For this contraction, push with everything you have." Sid glanced to Holly. "Be on standby."

Holly nodded. Bram sensed they weren't telling him everything that could happen, but he didn't want to scare Evie. Instead, he kissed her cheek and whispered, "You're strong, Evie Marshall. You took on a dragonman and captured his heart. You bloody well better not let a little high blood pressure take you down."

She answered through gritted teeth, "I'll keep that in minnnnn—aaahhhhh."

Evie screamed as her contraction hit.

Sid's voice was full of dominance as she ordered, "Push, Evie. Now."

Evie dug her nails into Bram's hand as she pushed. Given that her upper body was strapped to the bed in case she went into convulsions, it couldn't be easy.

Pushing aside his worry, he thought of love, strength, and the minute he could hug both Evie and their new baby close. He would remain positive even if it killed him.

Sid's voice rose over Evie's screaming. "You're doing well, Evie. When your contraction ends, I want you to stop pushing and rest."

Bram held his breath, hoping each second would bring the end of the latest contraction and relieve Evie's pain. Her screams would haunt him for the rest of his life. How any male went through this more than once, Bram had no bloody idea.

Evie went quiet and slumped onto the bed as if all of her energy had been sapped from her body. Careful to keep his worry from his voice, Bram murmured, "You did brilliantly, Evie. You really did."

Despite the exhaustion in her eyes and posture, Evie answered, "Nothing bloody happened. The baby isn't out yet."

He placed a hand on her forehead and strummed his thumb back and forth. "She just wants to make a grand entrance. She is a clan leader's daughter after all."

"It could be a boy, Bram."

"We could bet and then I can claim a prize later."

Evie's eyes drooped and then opened again. "I can't believe you're suggesting a bet when I can barely stay awake."

He grinned. "You're the one who didn't want to be coddled."

Holly's voice prevented Evie from replying. "Dr. Sid, you might want to see this."

Bram glanced up and the two females put their heads together in front of the vitals monitor. Bram's dragon spoke up. *I don't like it. Something's wrong. Demand to know what it is.*

And upset Evie? We can't do anything that might elevate her blood pressure. You know that.

His beast growled. *I hate not being able to do anything.*

I agree, although I don't plan on earning a medical degree, if you're thinking of suggesting it.

Sid turned toward them, her face neutral. "Evie, if we can't get at least the head out on this next push, it could be dangerous to both you and the baby's health. I need you to make this next contraction count. Can you do that?"

Evie's voice was faint as she answered, "Yes, I'll try. But please tell me what's wrong, Sid. I want to be prepared."

Sid answered, "While the medication is keeping your blood pressure stable, the level of dragon-shifter hormones in your body has spiked. If they rise much further, your blood pressure could shoot through the roof and send you into convulsions. But," Sid emphasized, "if we can get the baby out, I can start a course of treatment and everything should turn out fine. So draw on every bit of strength you possess and push on the next contraction. Understand?"

Evie nodded. "Yes."

As Sid turned to Holly and gave an order to bring another nurse, Bram stilled his thumb on Evie's forehead and his mate looked at him. Bram kept his voice soft, yet firm. "I order you not to push the baby out."

The corner of Evie's mouth ticked up. "You know I never follow any order you throw my way."

"Exactly."

Evie laughed and Bram's worry eased a fraction. His human was strong, stubborn, and a fighter. She would make it through the birth. She had to. He wouldn't accept anything less than a happy ending for his mate.

~ ~ ~

Evie debated keeping her eyes open to stare at Bram's loving face, but her exhaustion won out and they closed.

She was so bloody tired. Not only that, the magnesium sulfate was making her woozy and it was difficult to concentrate. If meeting her new baby wasn't incentive enough, getting off the damn medication and regaining her wits was another reason to get the baby out as soon as possible.

While Evie was trying to be strong, she wasn't sure how much longer she could keep pushing. If she were birthing a human baby, she could have drugs and a cesarean section. Unfortunately, both were out because of the baby being half dragon-shifter.

She would just have to fight a little while longer for her little dragon baby.

Pain started in her back and she braced herself. "Another contraction is coming."

Bram squeezed her hand at the same time as Sid repositioned herself between Evie's legs. "As soon as it starts, push, Evie."

The pain moved from her back to her lower belly and then it felt as if someone had reached inside her uterus and twisted.

Screaming helped her as she pushed with everything she had.

As parts of her stretched, she crushed Bram's hands in hers. The baby needed to come out. He or she just had to.

Sid's voice cut through the air. "The head is out. Come on, Evie. Push a little harder."

She wanted to tell Sid to try pushing a melon out of her vagina, but Bram kissed her cheek and she looked into his eyes. The love and strength she saw there gave her a little rush. Drawing on every iota of strength she had, Evie leaned her head back and pushed.

Something finally slipped free and a second later, Evie heard a baby's cry. Tears filled her eyes. Her baby was alive.

Sid shouted, "It's a girl," and Bram kissed her gently. "I told you it was a girl."

But Holly's voice prevented Evie from saying anything. "Dr. Sid."

Something beeped on the monitor. Evie asked, "Is it my baby girl? What's wrong?"

Sid handed off the baby to Holly and looked Evie directly into the eye. "Your baby is perfectly healthy. But, Evie, your blood pressure is spiking. With the baby out, I need to start a new course of treatment straight away. I'm sorry, but holding your baby is going to have to wait."

Bram growled out, "Then start the bloody treatment Sid. You're wasting time."

Evie looked to Bram and was about to tell him to go greet their daughter, but in the next second, Evie lost control of her body as she fell into a seizure.

~ ~ ~

The instant Evie's eyes rolled to the back of her head and she started convulsing, Bram's stomach dropped. "Evie."

Sid and her nurse jumped into action. As Sid issued orders and the nurse pushed something into Evie's IV, Bram kept his grip on his mate's hand. He drew on every bit of dominance he possessed and whispered, "You stay alive, Evie. Don't you even think of leaving me."

Sid moved to his side of the bed. "Move, Bram. Get out of the way."

While his beast snarled at the order, Bram forced himself to let go of Evie's hand and move back.

His dragon spoke up. *We should be with our mate. Why did you move?*

Sid knows what she's doing. She has the power to save Evie. We don't.

His beast fell silent and Bram watched as Sid and her male nurse talked about things he didn't understand. The second Evie stopped convulsing, he let out a breath. Surely that would be the end of it.

The monitor stopped beeping its warning, but Evie didn't wake up. Bram clenched his fingers and asked, "What's going on, Sid? Tell me."

Sid nodded at the nurse and turned toward him. "Evie's developed eclampsia, brought on mostly by the dragon-shifter hormones in her blood. I need to watch her closely and focus on bringing her vitals back to normal."

He stared at a motionless Evie. She was breathing, but her face was pale. "Just tell me straight up if I should be worried or not."

Sid gripped his shoulder. "Between Holly and me, Evie has the best chance she would have anywhere in the UK."

"That's not an answer."

"I don't do platitudes, Bram. You know that. It's more likely she'll be fine than not, but I can't say with certainty everything will be rosy. I'm going to keep her in an induced coma for the next twenty-four hours while I try to bring down her blood pressure and lower the dragon-shifter hormones in her system. The best thing you can do right now is spend time with your daughter."

Bram debated staying at Evie's side, but his dragon spoke up. *She's right. Our daughter is alone and a lot more helpless. Sid needs time to take care of our mate. Let's take care of our child and then we can spend time with Evie. Our mate would expect us to look after our young.*

Taking the five steps to Evie's bed, he leaned down and kissed Evie's lips. "I'm going to check on our daughter and be right back, love. I know how you wish your parents had been around more. I'll make sure our wee one knows she's loved from day one."

Evie's silence cut him to the bone. But then his daughter cried, and Bram forced himself to leave Evie's side.

Holly was just wrapping the wee one in a green blanket as Bram stopped next to her. Looking down, his daughter's eyes were closed while she cried. His dragon's instinct kicked in to take care of the baby, but Bram ignored his dragon to ask, "Can I hold her?"

With a smile, Holly gently lifted the baby and placed her in Bram's arms. Gently rocking back and forth, his daughter eventually stopped crying. He kissed her on the nose and whispered, "Welcome to the world, Eleanor Rose. I'm your daddy and I'm going to take care of you. Your mum needs to rest, or she'd be right here with me." He kissed Eleanor's little nose again. "We're not the only ones who have been waiting, though. As soon as I can manage it, you need to say hello to your older brother."

Holly's gentle voice filled his ear. "I can fetch Murray and bring him here whenever you want. I don't want the others to come in just yet with Evie until she's stable, but with the extra nurse in the room, I can spare five minutes to get Murray. Having both of your children together might help."

Bram managed to tear his eyes away from his daughter to look over at Evie. "The only thing that will help is having Evie back. But as a father, I need to be strong for my children. Bring Murray. He needs to meet his little sister."

With a nod, Holly told Sid what she was doing and left. Bram hugged wee Eleanor tighter against his body and breathed in her baby scent. He only hoped Evie could also cuddle their daughter before much longer.

Chapter Five

Evie felt as if she were drifting in the middle of an empty, black space. She couldn't move, but every once in a while she heard a low rumbling voice that sounded like Bram's. She wanted to ask him where he was, but every time she tried, she couldn't make her mouth form words.

It was so bloody frustrating for a woman used to demanding the truth.

After who the hell knew how long, a soft warmth touched her cheek and a scent of freshly laundered clothes and a comforting scent she couldn't name, mixed with Bram's, drifted into her nose.

Then a soft, wet something pressed against her cheek before Bram's voice filled her ear. "Evie Marie, wake up. The medication should be wearing off and your daughter is anxious to meet you." She tried to make her mouth work and failed. Bram's spoke again. "I saw your brows move, Evie. Come on, love, wake up."

She wanted to say she was trying, but couldn't get it out. Bram's warm, firm lips kissed hers and he murmured, "Don't wake up. That's an order and I expect you to follow it to the letter. Do you hear me?"

Oh, she heard him. And Evie wanted to kick him in the bollocks if he kept it up.

Bram's chuckle rolled over her. "That's my lass. Prove me wrong. Come on, now, I dare you."

No matter how much she tried, Evie couldn't open her eyes. It was frustrating being able to hear everything and do nothing.

She searched her mind for ideas, but soon, a baby's cry pierced the air. It shot straight to her heart. Her baby needed her.

The warmth from her cheek disappeared and she ached to cry out, "No." Instead, she mustered every bit of her stubbornness. Surely she could open her eyes a few millimeters. Eyelids weighed next to nothing.

Open, damn it. I want to see my baby.

Millimeter by millimeter, she moved her eyelids until the light hit them. She cried out and promptly closed her eyes again.

In the next instant, Bram's hand was on her cheek. "Evie, love, are you in pain? Holly, come check on her. Please."

Bram's touch vanished as another set of smaller, softer hands took her pulse. Then her right eye was open and the light hit again. However, this time, she could make out Holly's dark-haired form above her. Evie whispered, "Too bright."

Holly released her eyelid. "Right, then can you try to answer my questions? Either say 'yes' or if it's too difficult, wiggle your fingers of your left hand."

Concentrating, Evie tried to make her mouth work again. But after a few seconds of trying, she gave up and wiggled her fingers.

Holly's voice filled the room again. "Good. If you're in pain, wiggle your left hand again."

At this rate, she'd never see, let alone hold her daughter. Tired of the nonverbal form of communication, Evie growled and finally forced her mouth to work. "No pain."

Her daughter started crying again and Evie decided enough was enough. It was time to meet her baby.

Slowly blinking her eyes, Evie withstood the split second shock of light and continued blinking until her eyes adjusted. Her throat was dry and scratchy, but she didn't want to waste time asking for water. "Bram, where's our baby?"

Bram looked to Holly and the Scottish woman nodded. "Her vitals are much better. As long as Evie's not lying about the pain, you can have a few minutes whilst I fetch Dr. Sid." Holly looked down at her with stern eyes. "You are telling the truth, aren't you?"

Evie's voice was faint as she answered, "I'm sore between my legs, but nowhere else."

"Right, then I'll fetch Dr. Sid."

Holly left and Evie moved her gaze to the bright purple bundle in Bram's arms. "Can I see her?"

Bram smiled. "Evie Marie Marshall, I'd like for you to meet Eleanor Spidey-sense Moore-Llewellyn."

She frowned. "What?"

Bram winked. "Kidding. Say hello to Eleanor Rose."

He then lowered the bundle and held it right next to her.

As she studied the pink, wrinkly child, tears filled Evie's eyes. "We have a daughter."

Bram kept the baby resting on the bed next to her while he crouched down. "We do, Evie, we do. And she's been anxious to meet everyone, but I said no until you had a chance to see her."

Evie tried to lift her arms, but she was weak. "Can you bring her closer? I want to kiss her."

Bram gently moved Eleanor until she was right next to Evie's face. Once their daughter was situated, Bram moved his free hand to Evie's head and brushed the hair from her face.

Between Bram's gentle touch and the soft weight of her daughter next to her, tears rolled down the sides of Evie's cheeks.

Bram stilled his fingers. His voice was gentle as he asked, "What's wrong, love? Everything will be all right now. Sid said you're past any danger."

She sniffed, turned her head slightly and kissed her daughter's head. Then she murmured, "I'm just happy to be here in this moment." She kissed Eleanor again and looked back to Bram's gaze. "But what about Murray? He should be here, too."

Stroking her hair, Bram answered, "He was here earlier. But Mel and Tristan have been looking after him. From all their reports, wee Murray's been having a brilliant time with Jack and Annabel. So much so, he might not want to come home."

The door opened. Sid walked in with Holly right behind her. Sid glanced at the monitors before moving to Evie's other side. "It's good to have you back, Evie. I hate to tear you away from your first meeting with your daughter, but I really should do a thorough exam now that you're conscious."

Evie wanted to hug Eleanor close and never let her go. But the rational side of her brain knew she wasn't any good to anyone if she wasn't healthy. Kissing her daughter's soft fuzz of dark hair one more time, she answered, "Of course. You saved my life, Sid. I owe you nothing less than cooperation."

The corner of Sid's mouth ticked up. "I'm going to remind you of that in the future." Sid looked to Bram. "Take Eleanor and wait outside. I can't have Evie tensing or stressing if the baby cries." Bram opened his mouth to say something, but Sid cut him off. "No excuses. There are a few clan members outside waiting to talk with you, anyway. Kai's been doing the best he can, but politics and smooth-talking things over isn't exactly his forte. Not even Jane's influence has helped with that."

Evie looked up at her mate. "Go, Bram. The sooner I get healthy, the sooner I can go home and we can all be a family."

Bram kissed her one last time. "I love you, Evie."

"I love you, too."

Bram waved Eleanor's little hand goodbye and then her dragonman was gone. The room was emptier without Bram and Eleanor, but she would see them soon enough.

Looking to Sid, Evie asked, "How long will I need to stay in this hospital bed?"

Sid placed her fingers on Evie's wrist to take her pulse. A short time later, she answered, "That depends on if your blood pressure drops and remains stable or not. Regardless, you can start feeding your daughter soon. The harmful drugs should be out of your system by now."

Evie attempted to sit up. After Sid helped, she succeeded. "Thank you, Sid, for saving my life."

Sid waved a hand in dismissal. "I only did my job. Besides, it's not entirely altruistic on my part. Bram would have my head if anything ever happened to you."

Studying Sid's face, Evie realized how little she actually knew Stonefire's head doctor. Did she want her own children? Did she fancy anyone? What did she do for fun? Evie had no idea. Rumors about Sid's dragon being silent had been confirmed by Bram, but that wasn't any reason to give up hope on love. Evie had seen Sid's longing glances at some of the couples when Sid had thought no one else was looking, so she knew the doctor yearned for someone.

In that instant, Evie decided she would repay Sid saving her life by finding her a mate of her own. Evie needed to determine who was not only single, but also a good match. Hell, maybe she could even convince Bram to think about a human male. How she would accomplish that, Evie had no idea, but it was worth a shot.

Glad to have her mind functioning again, Evie complied with Sid's orders during the exam. The sooner she finished, the sooner she could hold Eleanor Rose for the first time in her arms.

~~~

Bram cuddled his daughter against his chest, took a deep breath, and walked out into the waiting area.

Instead of the rag-tag bunch of clan members waiting to have their grievances heard that he had expected, the room was filled with his closest friends.

Kai was the first one to reach him and squeezed his shoulder. "Congratulations, Bram."

Jane was at his side and held out her arms. "Can I hold her?"

Bram had wanted Mel and Tristan to be the first ones to hold Eleanor, but at the longing in Jane's voice, he couldn't help but answer, "Of course."

As he gently transferred the baby to Jane, the tall human cooed and stroked Eleanor's cheek. Jane then looked to Kai. "Your turn."

Kai frowned. "I'm not exactly a baby person."

"Of course you are. You just don't know it yet." Jane moved Eleanor until she supported the baby's head with one hand and her body with the rest. Bram itched to take his daughter back, but his dragon spoke up. *Kai will not hurt our child. He lives every day to protect the clan. Allow him a minute with our baby.*

If he wants a baby, he should have his own.

Judging by his female's actions, they soon will.

Bram knew Kai and Jane were waiting to have children so both of them could focus on their careers, but his beast had a point. *A minute, but no more.*

Tristan appeared at his side with Jack in one arm and Bram's son Murray in the other. "Bram."

Murray put out his arms. "Dada."

Unable to resist his son, Bram took Murray and bounced him in his arms. "Have you been a good lad?"

Murray nodded and Bram ruffled his son's dark hair. Then Murray asked, "Mama?"

"We'll visit Mum in a bit. Would you like to see your sister Eleanor again?"

Murray looked over at the bundle in Kai's arms. "Nor." Murray pointed. "Nor."

He chuckled. "I'll take that as a yes." The second Bram was close enough, Murray leaned over to stare at his sister. Bram took Murray's hand and guided it to gently brush Eleanor's cheek. "You're going to have to look out for her, Murray. You're the big brother. It's every dragonman's job to look out for their females."

Melanie appeared at his side with her daughter in her arms and shook her head. "Evie and I are going to have to work on your son. There are limits, you know. Tristan should know since he crossed them with Arabella."

Tristan grunted. "She's my sister. The day I stop wanting to protect her is the day I am no longer worthy of being her brother."

Mel's face softened. "There's that hidden sweetness again."

Before Bram could say anything, a voice he hadn't heard in nearly a year filled the room. "Bram."

Turning his head, Bram saw his younger brother, Bennett, along with Bram's niece, Ava. "Bennett."

Bram met his brother halfway and gave him a one-sided hug. Then his niece, Ava, tugged on his shirt and Bram crouched carefully with Murray in his arm to give his niece a hug, too.

Leaning back, he studied his niece's blue eyes. "You're nearly a grown dragonwoman."

Ava giggled. "I'm only seven-and-three-quarters."

"Aye, but you're going to be as tall as me before long." Bram stood up to smile at his brother. "I didn't think you'd be back yet. You could've called."

Bennett winked. "And ruin the surprise?"

Bram looked around for his sister-in-law. "Where's Shauna?"

Bennett's face turned neutral. "She's still back in Ireland. Her mother hasn't improved at all, but she sends her love."

Bram's brother had spent the last eleven months in Ireland to support his Irish mate, Shauna. Bram squeezed his brother's shoulder. "It's good to see you, brother." Sid exited the door on the far side of the room and Bram slapped his brother's shoulder one last time. "We'll catch up later, okay? I need to speak with the doctor and make sure Evie's okay."

Bennett nodded. "Of course. I need to find some dinner for me and Ava anyway. We haven't eaten since leaving Ireland."

Ava tugged her father's hand. "Look, it's Mr. MacLeod. Can we say hello, Dad? Please? He's so much better than my current teacher."

Bennett frowned. "Ava, you have a nice teacher back in Donegal."

Ava asked again, "Please?"

With a sigh, Bennett nodded. "Okay, if he's not too busy. But only for a few minutes."

60

Bennett headed toward Tristan, and Bram went up to Sid. As soon as he was close enough, he demanded, "Well?"

Sid raised an eyebrow. "That tone won't work on me, Bram. Why you keep trying to pull your dominance crap on me, I'll never understand."

Murray squirmed in Bram's arms. Automatically, he bounced his son. "Let's not do this dance again. How's Evie?"

Sid put her hands into the pockets of her white lab coat. "As long as there aren't any other complications, she should be discharged in a few days. While she can start seeing visitors, I want her to try feeding Eleanor first."

"Right, then take Murray whilst I get her."

Bram handed over Murray and headed to where Kai and Jane were standing. However, Melanie was currently holding Eleanor while Jane held a humming Annabel.

He put out his hands. "Sorry to disrupt the baby time, but I need to take Eleanor back to Evie."

Mel gently handed over the baby. "Is she doing better? Can we see her soon?"

"Believe me, once Evie starts seeing visitors, you'll be the first to know."

Mel nodded. "Just holler if you need us to watch Murray again."

Bram smiled and headed back to Sid. The dragonwoman laughed as she tickled the little boy's neck and it hit Bram that he rarely saw Sid so relaxed. He hadn't been checking in with his head doctor as often lately because of Evie, but he'd need to make sure Sid was doing okay as soon as possible. As much as it pained him to admit it, Sid always ran the risk of a breakdown because of her silent dragon.

Pushing aside the serious thoughts for the moment, he smiled at Sid. "The lad likes you."

Sid never looked up. "He's such a good little boy. I wish they were all like him."

Bram snorted. "You haven't seen one of his rare tempers."

Sid adjusted Murray on her hip. "That's your job, as the dad. But enough about your son, let's take care of Evie."

They wound through the corridors and into Evie's room. Her eyes were closed, but they opened a second later. Evie smiled as she reached out her arms. "Come here, Murray. Mama needs a cuddle."

Sid handed over the toddler and Murray lay against Evie's chest as she stroked his hair. The sight went straight to his heart; Evie would never treat Murray differently just because he was adopted.

Bram kissed the top of Evie's forehead and sat beside her on the bed. "Our family is finally all together."

Evie snuggled into his side. "I'm so happy right now that I might start crying again. Just warning you."

As Bram sat with his new family, his heart nearly burst with happiness. And, bloody hell, his eyes were misty. "Cry all you want, love. Having you alive along with my two children is making my eyes wet."

"Bram."

He merely sat in silence holding his daughter in one arm and his mate and son in the other.

CHAPTER SIX

Two Weeks Later

Evie adjusted the silky, blue swaddling cloth around Eleanor for the fifteenth time. The bloody thing never seemed to wrap around her daughter as neatly as when Holly or one of the other nurses did it.

Biting her bottom lip, Evie got creative and tied the extra fabric into a bow. "There we go. Mama made you pretty." Eleanor waved her arms and Evie sighed. "Okay, you look like a poorly wrapped Christmas present, but it'll have to do. We'll be late to the celebration if I unwrap you and try again."

Lifting her daughter into her arms, Evie added another blanket around her baby. The walk to the great hall wasn't long, but she wasn't taking any chances.

As soon as she descended the stairs, Bram came to greet her. He wore the traditional dragon-shifter outfit of a solid maroon-colored material held in place around her waist like a kilt and tossed over one shoulder. She spent an extra second studying her handsome mate and Bram chuckled. "I wish I could please my lusty female, but you haven't healed yet. You'll just have to undress me with your mind."

She met his eyes and frowned. "Just because I was admiring your muscled arms doesn't mean I was thinking about sex. I recently pushed a baby out of my vagina. It's going to be a short while before I feel in the mood, Bram."

Bram walked up to her and cupped her cheek. After giving her a gentle kiss, he murmured, "No worries, love. You're worth the wait."

Evie blinked back tears and rubbed them away with one arm. "I can't wait until these bloody hormones are out of my body. You think I would be back in charge of myself by now."

"I think it's adorable." Before Evie could reply, Bram lightly brushed Eleanor's cheek. "As are you, wee princess."

She watched Bram coo over their daughter and she let out a contented sigh. "Do we really have to go out tonight? I'm more than happy to stay in with you and our two babies."

Bram met her gaze again. "Not only do we need to officially present our daughter to the clan, it's Stonefire's first combined Christmas and Winter Solstice celebration. Melanie expects you to be there."

"I had fully intended to be giving birth right about now. Just my luck Eleanor was born two weeks early."

Bram moved to place an arm around her shoulders and squeezed. "Come, love. Presenting a new baby is a big tradition for Stonefire. You don't have to stay the whole night, but thirty minutes will mean the world to everyone waiting."

They started walking. "I know. It's just that I haven't had a full night's sleep since we brought Eleanor home. I usually like chatting with the clan members, but I'm crabby and will probably bite their heads off instead."

Bram paused by the door to pluck Evie's dark grey cloak off the wall and settled it around her shoulders. "Every parent in attendance will understand." Bram grinned. "Besides, I know how you love surprises and I have one for you after the ceremony."

She looked at him askance. "It depends on the surprise."

"You'll like this one, I promise."

Since Bram's track record with good surprises was about fifty-fifty, Evie wondered what in the world he could've done this time. She wasn't big on presents, as he well knew. There were only a handful of things she truly wanted, and they were mostly people missing from her life.

Then it hit her—there was one person she'd been trying to locate for nearly a year. "Did you find Alice? Is she here?"

Bram nodded toward the door. "Come and find out for yourself."

Evie hoped it was true. Alice Darby was the only friend she'd had for most of her life. Alice had also been the only one who had understood Evie's fascination with the dragon-shifters. Yet she'd been unable to get a hold of her friend for far too long. Every day that passed in silence caused Evie's stomach to twist in fear.

Eleanor snuggled against Evie and it helped to relax her. Looking at her daughter, she whispered, "Okay, I get your hint. You want Daddy to hurry up and tell us about the surprise so you can go back to sleep."

Bram snorted. "Nice try, Evie." He pressed against Evie's lower back. "Come, love. It's show time."

With a sigh, Evie tucked Eleanor's blanket tighter around her tiny body and exited their cottage toward the great hall.

~~~

How Bram had managed to keep his secret from Evie, he didn't know. His bloody dragon was irritating the hell out of him.

His beast spoke up. *She will be pleased. We should tell her. Then she'd look forward to the celebration.*

For the tenth time, I like watching Evie's face when I surprise her. And this one is a good one. It's the best Solstice present I could give her.

His dragon huffed. *I still say she deserves more presents.*

She isn't a dragon-shifter. Evie doesn't have to worry about pleasing her spoiled other half.

Thankfully, his beast faded into the back of his mind. The tales about dragons loving treasures hit a little too close to home sometimes.

Bram glanced down at his daughter and hugged Evie closer against him. If only Murray were in his arms, the moment would be perfect. "I hope wee Murray hasn't tired out my brother. Ava is a handful by herself, but adding Murray to the mix creates chaos."

Evie smiled. "Murray needs time to get to know his uncle and cousin. Besides, if Bennett can handle Ava, then he'll be fine. I'm more worried about Eleanor growing up like her female cousin. Two hyperactive children will be the death of me."

Kissing Evie's hair, he murmured, "We'll manage, love. We'll manage."

They arrived at the towering brick building that served as Stonefire's great hall. Lights shone from the windows and music drifted out into the air from the doorway. Five seconds later, Melanie rushed out of the hall right toward them. As soon as she was close enough, Mel asked, "What took you so long? The ceremony is due to start in a few minutes. Jane worked hard to invite a few friends from the press as well as set-up equipment to record the event. You know she's due to start her podcast series after the New Year and wants to include tonight in one of the first episodes."

Evie's voice was dry as she replied, "We're not all super mums like you, Melanie Hall-MacLeod. You might've been able to start working weeks after birthing the twins, but I'm still trying to keep my blood pressure under control. In fact, you shouldn't do anything to try and raise it."

Even in the half-darkness, Evie made out the twinkle in Bram's eyes. "Aye, Evie's right. Maybe we'll take our time to the hall."

Evie looked up at Bram and raised an eyebrow. "As if you should talk. You're the one going on about surprises."

Mel jumped in. "Come on, Evie. You don't want to keep little Eleanor out in the cold, do you?"

"Damn you, Melanie."

Melanie grinned. "Thanks to you, I'm pretty good at all the shortcuts for hitting a mother's guilt by now. If you didn't want me to use them on you, then you shouldn't have used them on me."

Evie grunted. "If it were anyone else, Mel, I would tell them to stuff it."

Mel winked. "But you love me too much."

As Evie shook her head, Bram's dragon growled and he knew he'd better do something or his bloody beast would give him a headache. "Fine, we'll go. Just give us a minute."

Melanie looked from Bram to Evie and back again. "One minute. Then I'll send Tristan and Kai to get you."

"Kai won't do anything to order me around," Bram stated.

Melanie tilted her head. "If it's to please Jane, then yes, he sure as hell will."

Bram sighed. While he was happy his head Protector had found a second chance at love, Bram kept finding out new things about his head of security. If Bram wasn't careful, Jane would be the one giving orders.

But he'd have a chat with the human female later. "Go tell them we're coming, lass."

With a nod, Mel turned and went back inside the great hall. Bram brushed Evie's cheek. "Give me a kiss, love. Then we can go inside and finish the bloody ceremony."

Evie smiled. "You've changed your tune."

Not wanting to admit it, Bram gently kissed Evie. But the second his lips touched her soft mouth, his dragon demanded more.

Biting her bottom lip, Evie opened and he stroke his tongue against hers. Tasting her was a bad idea as he wanted her with every atom of his being; yet according to Dr. Sid, he couldn't have her for at least another six weeks.

After one last stroke, Bram broke the kiss and whispered, "Now you'll have my taste in your mouth."

"And this is important why?"

"Because all of those males will be staring at you. Between your beautiful body and the baby in your arms, more than one is going to wish they could claim you."

Evie rolled her eyes. "I thought the possessiveness was supposed to ease after the birth of our daughter."

He lightly slapped her arse. "With you, Evie Marshall, it's never going to fade."

Before his mate could say another word, Bram guided them into the hall. He'd taken a little bit of time for himself, but as leader, he also needed to think of the clan. There was no better way to celebrate the end of the year than with a new birth and a welcoming ceremony.

LOVED BY THE DRAGON

~~~

As Evie gently bounced Eleanor in her arms, she scanned the crowd for Alice's face. But after a thorough search, she didn't spot her friend. While Evie knew it'd been a long shot, she really had hoped Bram's surprise had been finding her friend. Especially since Evie already had everything else she wanted at Stonefire—a family, friends, and a purpose.

While temporarily on leave from her duties to take care of her daughter, Evie had been working with the Department of Dragon Affairs more and more lately. The agency was still rebuilding after the bombing earlier in the year, but that didn't mean Evie wasn't going to tap her contacts to try and get Stonefire the best deals she could.

She also needed to keep an ear out for who was going to be the next Director of the DDA. One man in particular had the greatest chance, but Evie would walk through Hell barefoot before she allowed Jonathan Christie to take control. That man hated dragon-shifters and would be nothing but trouble.

Before her mind could wander further about how she could stop Christie, Bram's voice boomed through the hall. "Thank you all for coming. I know tonight is all about the dual celebration of Christmas and the Winter Solstice. However, I'm adding on to the agenda to celebrate the birth of my daughter, Eleanor Rose."

The crowd cheered. Evie smiled as Bram put an arm around her waist. He continued, "Before Evie takes wee Eleanor down to the main floor so each of you have the chance to touch the baby's swaddling in welcome, let's have Stonefire's silversmith and chief artist, Dylan Turner, come to the stage so that he can present Eleanor Rose with her future tattoo design."

The crowd parted as Dylan made his way toward Evie and Bram.

Evie had yet to witness a baby's welcoming ceremony. However, she did know that the silversmith designed a unique tattoo design for each new child. Dylan had records going back hundreds of years and had created something original yet related to Evie and Bram for their daughter.

Dylan ascended the dais carrying a large placard covered with a cloth as well as a smaller package wrapped nearly in a baby's blanket. The brown-haired man in his early forties presented the smaller one to Bram. As Bram took it, Dylan stated, "May your child grow and flourish so that she may receive the gift of my tattoo design on her sixteenth birthday."

Bram gave the customary reply. "She will proudly display your work to the world."

Dylan nodded, which signaled for Bram to untie the ribbon and remove the purple and blue blanket covering. Inside was a framed copy of Eleanor's tattoo. While the curls in the design reminded Evie of Bram's tattoo, there were also sharp, jagged points woven throughout. There was probably meaning in the design, but Evie would ask Bram about it later.

For now, Bram looked to Dylan again. "Thanks, friend. We will treasure this. Please share your gift with the clan."

Dylan removed the cloth from the nearly five-foot placard, turned it around and held it up. The clan clapped and cheered. Evie could clearly hear, "Welcome, Eleanor!" from several of the louder clan members.

She half-expected Eleanor to start crying, but her daughter merely squirmed.

Bram finally raised a hand and the hall quieted again. "Now that we've welcomed my daughter, Evie and I will greet you all on the floor so you can say hello."

Bram nodded one last time at Dylan before placing his hand on Evie's lower back. As they descended the stairs, he whispered, "Survive this, Evie Marie, and I can finally give you your present."

Evie opened her mouth to reply, but the clan members were already lining up to welcome little Eleanor. Saving her questions for later, Evie smiled and played the role of a clan leader's mate. The sooner she finished this task, the sooner she could find out what in the bloody hell Bram was lording over her.

CHAPTER SEVEN

An hour later, Bram finally managed to get Evie out of the great hall and into one of the side offices in the same building. Their hungry daughter was crying. Even though some of the clan had yet to give their official greetings, no one wanted to deny the baby her dinner.

The second Bram shut the door, Evie took out her left breast and rearranged Eleanor until the child latched onto her nipple. The sight of his child at Evie's breast warmed both man and beast.

His dragon spoke up. *Our young is healthy and growing fast. Eleanor will catch the eye of every dragon-shifter when she's of age.*

Let's not think about our wee daughter's teenage years just yet. I want to enjoy the present.

It will come faster than you think. We should prepare and have plans in place to chase off those unworthy of Eleanor.

Bram chuckled. *I'm sure we can think of some interesting ways to scare off the males.*

Evie's voice interrupted his thoughts. "What did your dragon say to make you chuckle?"

Bram waved a hand. "Oh, just how he wants to scare away males when Eleanor is older."

Evie grinned. "I can get on board with that, especially if it's a growly dragonman."

He raised an eyebrow. "Human males are just as randy as dragon-shifters."

"I'm not so sure about that."

Neither one of them mentioned how dragon-shifter females still couldn't legally mate human males. Of course, knowing his Evie, she'd find a way to make it work if Eleanor fell for a human.

Touching his daughter's head, Bram met Evie's eyes and they shared a moment. There was something extremely intimate and precious about spending time alone with his mate and new daughter as Eleanor nursed.

His dragon growled. *Don't forget about Evie's surprise.*

Taking out his mobile phone with his free hand, Bram broke the silence. "Once Eleanor's fed, are you ready for your surprise?"

"Do you really need to ask that question?"

He shrugged. "Hey, you're the one who said she might be tired after half an hour. I'm just looking out for my mate."

Evie shook her head. "Sometimes, I wonder how I put up with you."

He leaned over and gently kissed her. "Because you love me."

She sighed. "Yes, it's true. But I have my limits. I want to know what you've been hiding from me."

Bram sent a text message and then looked back to Evie. "Give it ten minutes, love. Feed our daughter and then I can take her whilst you enjoy the surprise."

Evie studied him a second before saying, "You're a tease, Bram Moore-Llewellyn."

"Bloody right I am. But you love me anyway."

As he and his mate smiled at one another, Bram only hoped Evie wouldn't kill him later. In time, she'd appreciate his surprise.

In the short term, however, she might smack him in the bollocks with a cricket bat the first chance she had.

~~~

When Eleanor was fed and burped, Evie handed over the baby to Bram. "Well? Where's my surprise?"

"It's waiting next door."

Bram held Eleanor against his shoulder with one hand and opened the door. Exiting the room, Evie's heart thumped inside her chest.

Once upon a time, she'd hated surprises. Mostly because every surprise up until she'd met Bram had been a disappointment. Finding out she wasn't compatible to sacrifice herself to a dragon; losing most of her so-called friends after joining the DDA; or, most importantly, her parents' decision to move to Spain years ago because of the threats they'd received because of Evie's DDA job.

But she trusted Bram. He would never do anything to hurt her. Hell, he'd executed a rescue mission to save her from the dragon hunters earlier in the year. He would die rather than cause her pain.

Right, Evie. Get a grip. After taking a deep breath, Evie opened the door to the adjacent room and was greeted by the sight of someone she hadn't seen in over five years. "Mum."

A woman in her late fifties with red hair streaked with gray turned toward her and gave a weak smile. "Hello, Evie."

Evie looked from her mum to Bram and back again. "What? How? I don't understand."

Bram nudged her with his shoulder. "Just give your mum five minutes. If after that, you want her to leave, Kai will escort her away. I'll be waiting just outside the door."

Before Evie could do more than blink, Bram had closed the door behind him and Evie was alone with her mother.

She clenched her fingers as she tried to figure out what to say to the woman who had run away to Spain and never looked back.

Evie's mum, Karen, reached out a hand and then retreated. "You have quite the persuasive husband, Evie. He really does love you."

"He's my mate. And yes, he does."

"Evie…"

She put up a hand. "Don't, Mum. Just tell me why you're here now. I haven't heard from you since you left the country five years ago."

Her mum clenched a fist over her heart. "I wanted to come, I did. But your father was dead set against it. He'd lost his job, his friends, and nearly his life because of your career choice. The harassments and death threats never ceased and would've continued if we stayed in England."

Evie shook her head. "That's not an excuse. I asked several times if you could handle what would happen if I joined the DDA, and both of you assured me that you could." Her throat closed up and Evie closed her eyes a second before she continued, "We were never really close as a family, and I'd accepted that. But father disowned me and said you two didn't have a daughter anymore." Evie opened her eyes. "And that hurt."

"Believe me, love, I tried to change his mind. But you know how your father is. His word is final. Not even you and your arguments could ever persuade him to alter his decision."

Memories of heated arguments filled her mind and Evie forced them away. "And now, Mother? What did he say about you coming?"

Karen took a step toward her. "He forbade me to come. He didn't want me to risk my life."

"Then how are you here?"

Her mother took another step toward her. "I'd had enough. I wanted to see my daughter and grandchildren. He wouldn't allow it, so I left him."

Some of Evie's anger melted away. "Oh, Mum."

Tears filled Karen's eyes. "It took me a long time to realize and accept that he'd changed from the man I fell in love with. I finally did what was right and chose you, Evie Marie." Her mum opened her arms. "Will you forgive me?"

She paused a second before replying, "That depends. Are you really going to stick by me and my new family? It won't be easy. Our clan is at the forefront of trying to change the status quo for dragon-shifters and that brings danger."

Her mother nodded and lowered her arms. "I'm here for good this time, Evie. As long as you accept me. Those were Bram's terms."

"What terms?"

"I can have permission to stay on Stonefire for as long as Bram allows it." Karen patted her jacket pocket. "I have the paperwork right here. All it needs is Bram's signature."

Evie tried to digest everything that had happened. If her mother had permission papers, then Bram had been working on bringing her mother to Stonefire for a while.

As she stared at her mum's pale, round face and bloodshot eyes, Evie could tell the decision to come to Stonefire hadn't been easy. A small part of her wanted to envelop Karen Marshall in a hug and never let go.

But Evie didn't want to put herself or her children through heartbreak. She needed to be certain of her mother's intentions first. "If you stay, then you'll rarely be allowed off the clan's lands without a dragon-shifter escort or two. Any friends or family you have will need to go through the Home Secretary's office to obtain visitation passes. And, most importantly, if you run back to Dad, Stonefire won't offer you any protection. You'll be on your own."

It might sound a bit harsh, but Evie needed to protect her clan first and foremost. They had become her family.

Karen tilted her head. "If that means I can get to know my daughter better, then it's worth it, Evie. I will go through any test you toss my way. I'm staying for good this time."

Her mother's tone was confident. Evie couldn't remember her mother speaking with such conviction since Evie had been a child.

Karen opened her arms again. "Come here, my little angel. I've missed you."

At her mother's pet name for her as a little girl, tears pricked her eyes. Rushing into her mother's arms, Evie hugged her tight and whispered, "Please don't hurt me again, Mum. I don't think I can take it."

Karen leaned back and took Evie's face in her hands. "Never again, Evie. Never again." Her mother smiled. "Now how about you show me my grandchildren? And, hopefully, somewhere to stay. I'm not sure if dragon-shifters like to sleep outside, but it's bloody cold out there. All I want is a warm fire, my daughter, and my grandchildren for Christmas."

Evie smiled. "I may threaten Bram with sending him to sleep outside from time to time, but dragons hate the cold. Well, at least, my dragonman hates the cold." Evie wiped her eyes. "Bram, I know you can hear me, so come in."

Karen blinked as Bram opened the door with little Eleanor asleep in his arms. Her mate looked at Evie and her mother before asking, "So? Is my surprise a good one or a bad one?"

Evie gave her mum one last squeeze before turning toward Bram. "Since you heard every word, I'm not sure why you're asking. Gloating isn't good for you."

Bram put on a fake look of innocence. "I can't read your mind. Can't you tell me?" He changed his voice into a mock female one. "Oh, Bram. It's the best present ever. I'm going to have to find many ways to reward you."

Evie walked over to him and smacked his side. "I don't sound like that."

Karen jumped in. "Pardon, but how could he hear us?"

Evie lightly patted Bram's chest. "Dragon-shifters have supersensitive hearing. Unless a room is soundproofed or encased in thick steel, they can hear most conversations." Evie looked back to her mother. "So, be careful what you say. Dragon-shifters gossip worse than humans, in my opinion."

Bram chuckled. "Keep telling yourself that, love. Maybe someday it will actually be true."

Evie gently took Eleanor from Bram and whispered to her daughter, "Promise me you won't take after daddy. You know you want to be level-headed like me."

Bram snorted, but Evie ignored him and walked over to Karen. Her mother touched Eleanor's cheek and started crying. "She's beautiful, Evie."

Evie barely kept herself from crying. "Eleanor Rose, meet your grandmother."

Karen asked, "Can I hold her?"

As if Eleanor could understand the importance of the moment, she let out a sound that only meant one thing—a dirty nappy. "If you take her, you change her."

Karen nodded. "I can do that. Let me hold her."

As Evie handed her daughter over to Karen, Bram appeared at her side. "My master plan is working. Now I won't have to change so many nappies."

Karen smiled. But Evie beat her mum to the reply. "Just for that, Mum and I will take half of them and you get the other half."

Bram frowned. "That's unfair."

Evie grinned. "Then you'll just have to find a way to convince me to change the percentages."

Bram pulled her close. "I think I can do that." He gave a long, lingering kiss before he whispered, "But most of that is going to have to wait until your mum isn't in the room."

Evie laughed and turned her head toward her mother. Between the warmth of being in her dragonman's arms and the sight of her mother holding her daughter, Evie was bursting with happiness. There was only one thing missing. "Mum, come home with us. You can stay with us until everything's settled. After you change Eleanor, we'll pick up your grandson, Murray, and you can meet him, too."

Karen's eyes were full of hope. "You want me to stay with you?"

Evie nodded. "For a little while, at least. I could use the extra help."

Bram squeezed Evie gently. "So, you still haven't answered my question. Do you like your surprise?"

She looked back into Bram's light blue eyes. "It's definitely in the top five best surprises."

"Top five?"

"Well, finding out I was your true mate was the best one, Bram. None of this would've happened without it."

The corner of his mouth ticked up. "I think I like that answer."

His lips descended on hers. Not caring that her mother was in the room, Evie melted into the kiss.

She thought mating her dragonman had been the best day of her life. But with each passing day, her life became happier and her love for him grew stronger.

It seemed that with Bram, her happy ending wasn't found in a day. No, it was for an entire lifetime.

Dear Reader:

Thanks for reading *Loved by the Dragon*. I hope you enjoyed this follow-up to Bram and Evie's story. They will, of course, keep appearing throughout future books, so keep an eye for them! Also, if you liked their story, please leave a review. Thank you!

The next book will be about Nikki Gray and Rafe Hartley and is entitled, *Surrendering to the Dragon*. It's a full-length book and is available in paperback. However, I would suggest reading the first book in the Lochguard spinoff series first. Turn the page for the synopsis and an excerpt from the first book in the Lochguard series, *The Dragon's Dilemma*.

To stay up to date on my latest releases, don't forget to sign-up for my newsletter at www.jessiedonovan.com/newsletter.

With Gratitude,
Jessie Donovan

The Dragon's Dilemma
(Lochguard Highland Dragons #1)

In order to pay for her father's life-saving cancer treatment, Holly Anderson offers herself up as a sacrifice and sells the vial of dragon's blood. In return, she will try to bear a Scottish dragon-shifter a child. While the dragonman assigned to her is kind, Holly can't stop looking at his twin brother. It's going to take everything she has to sleep with her assigned dragonman. If she breaks the sacrifice contract and follows her heart, she'll go to jail and not be able to take care of her father.

Even though he's not ready to settle down, Fraser MacKenzie supports his twin brother's choice to take a female sacrifice to help repopulate the clan. Yet as Fraser gets to know the lass, his dragon starts demanding something he can't have—his brother's sacrifice.

Holly and Fraser fight the pull between them, but one nearly stolen kiss will change everything. Will they risk breaking the law and betraying Fraser's twin? Or, will they find a way out of the sacrifice contract and live their own happily ever after?

Excerpt from *The Dragon's Dilemma*:

CHAPTER ONE

Holly Anderson paid the taxi driver and turned toward the large stone and metal gates behind her. Looking up, she saw "Lochguard" spelled out in twisting metal, as well as some words written in a language she couldn't read.

The strange words only reminded her of where she was standing—at the entrance to the Scottish dragon-shifter clan lands.

Taking a deep breath, Holly willed her stomach to settle. She'd signed up for this. In exchange for trying to conceive a dragon-shifter's child, Clan Lochguard had given her a vial of dragon's blood. The money from the sale of that dragon's blood was funding her father's experimental cancer treatments.

All she had to do was spend the next six months sleeping with a dragon-shifter. If she didn't conceive, she could go home. If she did, then she would stay until the baby was born.

What was a minimum of six months of her life if it meant her father could live?

That's if you don't die giving birth to a half-dragon-shifter baby.

Readjusting the grip on her suitcase, Holly pushed aside the possibility. From everything she'd read, great scientific strides were being made when it came to the role dragon hormones played on a human's body. If she were lucky, there might even be a way to prevent her from dying in nine to fifteen months' time, depending on the date of conception.

This isn't work. Stop thinking about conception dates and birthing babies. After all, she might luck out and never conceive at all.

Holly moved toward the front entrance and took in the view of the loch off to the side. The dull color of the lake's surface was calm, with rugged hills and mountains framing it. Considering she was in the Scottish Highlands in November, she was just grateful that it wasn't raining.

She wondered if it was raining back in Aberdeen.

Thinking of home and her father brought tears to her eyes. He was recovering well from his first course of cancer treatments, but her father's health could decline at any moment. If only dragon's blood could cure cancer, then she wouldn't have to worry.

But since cancer was one of the illnesses dragon's blood couldn't cure, surely the Department of Dragon Affairs would grant her another few weeks to help take care of her father if she asked.

As the taxi backed down the drive, Holly turned around and flagged for the driver to come back. However, before she could barely raise a hand, a voice boomed from the right. "Lass, over here."

She turned toward the voice and a tall, blond man waved her over with a smile.

Between his wind-tousled hair, twinkling eyes, and his grin, the man was gorgeous.

Not only that, he'd distracted her from doing something daft. If Holly ran away before finishing her contract, she'd end up in jail. And then who would take care of her father?

The man motioned again. "Come, lass. I won't bite."

When he winked, some of Holly's nervousness faded. Despite the rumors of dragon-shifters being monsters, she'd followed the news stories over the last year and knew Lochguard was one of the good dragon clans. Rumors even said the Lochguard dragons and the local humans had once set up their own sacrifice system long before the British government had implemented one nationwide.

It was time to experience the dragon-shifters firsthand and learn the truth.

Pushing her shoulders back, Holly put on her take no-crap nurse expression and walked over to the dragonman. When she was close enough, she asked, "Who are you?"

The man grinned wider. "I'm glad to see you're not afraid of me, lass. That makes all of this a lot easier."

Before she could stop herself, Holly blurted, "Are you really a dragon-shifter?'

The dragonman laughed. "Aye, I am. I'm the clan leader, in fact. The name's Finn. What's yours?"

The easygoing man didn't match the gruff picture she'd conjured up inside her head over the past few weeks.

Still, dragons liked strength, or so her Department of Dragon Affairs counselor had advised her. Her past decade spent as a maternity nurse would serve her well—if she could handle frantic fathers and mothers during labor, she could handle anything. "You're not a very good clan leader if you don't know my name."

Finn chuckled. "I was trying to be polite, Holly." He lowered his voice to a whisper. "Some say we're monsters that eat bairns for breakfast. I was just trying to assure you we can be friendly."

Confident the smiling man wouldn't hurt her for questioning him, she stated, "You could be acting."

"I think my mate is going to like you."

At the mention of the word "mate," Holly's confidence slipped a fraction. After all, she'd soon be having sex with a dragon-shifter to try to conceive a child. That was the price all sacrifices had to pay.

And there was always a small chance she turned out to be the dragon-shifter's true mate. If that happened, she might never be able to see her father again. Dragons were notoriously possessive. She didn't think they'd let a mate go once they found one.

Finn's voice interrupted her thoughts. "Let me take that suitcase, Holly. The sooner we get you to my place, the sooner we can settle you in and answer some of your questions."

Finn put out a hand and she passed the case over. She murmured, "Thank you."

"Considering that you're helping my clan more than you know, the least I can do is carry a bag."

She eyed the tall dragonman. "You don't have to comfort me. I know what I volunteered to do."

Finn raised a blond eyebrow. "You looked about ready to bolt or cry a few minutes ago. I think a little kindness wouldn't hurt."

He was right, not that she would admit to it. After all, she was supposed to be strong.

Holly motioned toward the gates. "How about we go so you can give me the spiel and then let me meet my dragonman?"

The dragonman's smile faded. "So you're giving orders to me now, aye?"

Even though Holly was human, she still sensed the dominance and strength in his voice. She could apologize and try to hide her true self, but that would be too tiring to keep up long term. Instead, she tilted her head. "I'm used to giving orders. In my experience, as soon as a woman goes into labor, her other half goes crazy. If I don't take charge, it could put the mother's life as well as the child's in danger. I'm sure you've read my file and should know what to expect."

The corner of Finn's mouth ticked up. "Aye, I have. But I like to test the waters with potential clan members."

"I'm not—"

Finn cut her off. "Give it time, lass. You may well become one in the long run."

Without another word, Finn started walking. Since he was at least eight inches taller than her, she had to half-jog to catch up to him. However, before she could reply, another tall, muscled dragonman approached. He still had the soft face of late adolescence and couldn't be more than twenty.

The younger dragon-shifter motioned a thumb behind him. "Archie and Cal are at it again. If you don't break it up, they might shift and start dropping each other's cattle for the second time this week."

Finn sighed. "I should assign them a full-time babysitter."

The younger man grinned. "You tried that, but my grandfather escaped, as you'll remember."

"That's because he's a sneaky bastard." Finn looked to Holly. "This is Jamie MacAllister. He'll take you to my mate, Arabella. She can help you get settled before you meet Fergus."

"Who's Fergus?" Holly asked, even though she had a feeling she knew.

Finn answered, "Fergus MacKenzie is my cousin, but he's also your assigned dragonman."

Of course she'd be given the cousin of the clan leader. After all, Holly was the first human sacrifice on Lochguard in over a decade. They'd want to keep tabs on her.

Holly didn't like it, but since she had yet to meet this Fergus, she wouldn't judge him beforehand. For all she knew, Fergus MacKenzie might be a shy, quiet copy of his cousin.

Maybe.

Not sure what else to do, Holly nodded. After giving a few more orders, Finn left to address the problem and Jamie smiled down at her. "There's never a dull moment here, lass. Welcome to Lochguard."

Holly wasn't sure if that was a warning or a welcome.

~~~

Fraser MacKenzie watched his twin brother from the kitchen. His brother, Fergus, was due to meet his human sacrifice in the next few hours and instead of celebrating his last hours of freedom, Fergus was doing paperwork.

Sometimes, Fraser wondered how they were related at all.

Taking aim, he lobbed an ice cube across the room. It bounced off his brother's cheek and Fraser shouted, "Goal."

Frowning, Fergus glanced over. "Don't you have a hole to dig? Or, maybe, some nails to pound?"

Fraser shrugged a shoulder and inched his fingers toward another ice cube. "I finished work early. After all, it's not every day your twin meets the possible mother of his child."

As Fraser picked up his second ice cube, his mother's voice boomed from behind him. "Put it down, Fraser Moore MacKenzie. I won't have you breaking something if you miss."

He looked at his mother and raised his brows. "I never miss."

Clicking her tongue, his mother, Lorna, moved toward the refrigerator. "Stop lying to me, lad. You missed a step and now have the scar near your eye to prove it."

Fraser resisted the urge to touch his scar. "That was because my sister distracted me." He placed a hand over his heart. "I was just looking out for the wee lass."

Lorna rolled her eyes. "Faye was sixteen at the time and you were too busy glaring at one of the males."

"He was trouble. Faye deserved better," Fraser replied.

Fergus looked up from his paperwork. "Where is Faye?"

Lorna waved a hand. "The same as every day. She leaves early in the morning and I don't see her again until evening."

Fraser sobered up. "I wish she'd let us help her. Does anyone know if she can fly again yet?"

His younger sister, Faye, had been shot out of the sky by an electrical blast nearly two months earlier while in dragon form and her wing had been severely damaged. While she was no longer in a wheelchair, the doctors weren't sure if Faye would ever fly again.

His mother turned toward him. "I trust Arabella to help her. Faye will come to us when she's ready."

Jumping on the chance to lighten the mood again, Fraser tossed the ice cube into the sink and added, "I'm more worried about Fergus right now anyway. Who spends their last few hours of freedom cooped up inside? Even if he doesn't want to go drinking, he could at least go for a flight."

Fergus lifted the papers in his hand. "For your information, this is all of the new procedures and suggestions from the Department of Dragon Affairs. Finn worked hard to make Lochguard one of the trial clans for these new rules, and I'm not about to fuck it up." Lorna clicked her tongue and Fergus added, "Sorry, Mum."

Lorna leaned against the kitchen counter. "I still applaud you for what you're doing, Fergus. After the last fifteen years of near-isolation, the clan desperately needs some new blood."

Fergus shrugged a shoulder. "It's not a guarantee. Besides, how could I pass up the chance to help our cousin?"

Fraser rolled his eyes. "Right, you're being all noble when I know for a fact you just want to, er," he looked to his mum and back to Fergus, "sleep with a human lass."

"No one around here has stirred a mate-claim frenzy and I'm not about to look in the other clans. I'm needed here," Fergus replied. "A human sacrifice is my only other chance."

"And what if she's not your true mate, brother? Then what?" Fraser asked.

"I'll still try to win her over. If she gives me a child, I want to try to convince the human to stay."

Lorna spoke up. "Her father's ill, Fergus. Let's see how things go before you start planning the human's future." Lorna looked to Fraser. "Let's just hope she has spirit. I can handle anything but fear."

Fraser answered, "If Finn picked her out, then we should trust that he chose a good one."

"You're right, son," Lorna answered. She waved toward the living room. "Now, go get that ice cube."

"Fergus is closer. He could just toss it over."

Fergus looked back at his stack of papers. "Get it yourself."

With a sigh, Fraser moved toward the living room. "You were always a lazy sod."

Fergus looked up. "Takes one to know one. But at least this lazy sod is about to get his own cottage."

Lorna's voice drifted into the living room. "It's about time. One down, two more to go."

Fraser scooped up the ice cube and faced his mother. "Don't worry, Mum. You'll always have me. If I'm lucky, I won't have a mate until I'm fifty."

Fergus chimed in. "She'll kick you out on your arse before then."

"I'm feeling the love, brother."

Fergus looked up with a grin. "Someone has to love you, you unlovable bastard."

Tossing the ice cube into the sink, Fraser dried his hands. "You know you'll miss me, Fergus. I give it a week and then you'll be begging for my company."

"We'll see, Fraser. If I'm lucky, I'll be spending a week in my sacrifice's bed."

The thought of not seeing his twin every day did something strange to his heart. Brushing past it, Fraser headed toward the door. "As much as I'd love to stay and watch you read boring protocol, I'm going to watch some paint dry instead."

Fergus raised an auburn eyebrow. "What happened to spending time with your brother?"

"I never said anything about spending time with you. I wanted to show you a good time. The offer's still open if you're interested."

Shaking his head, Fergus answered, "Your good times always result in us waking up in strange places and not remembering the night before. I think I'll stay here."

Fraser shrugged. "Your loss." He looked to his mum. "I'll be home for dinner, don't worry."

Lorna answered. "You'd better be. Finn wants us to have a quiet dinner with Holly and help ease her into her new life here."

"Quiet is a bit of a stretch."

Lorna picked up an apple and tossed it at his head. Once he caught it, she answered, "Just get your arse home on time."

Fraser winked. "I'll try my best, but you know how the lasses love me."

Not wanting to hear his mother's lecture about settling down for the hundredth time, Fraser ducked out the front door.

While the human wouldn't be over to their house until dinnertime, she was due to arrive on Lochguard at any moment. He had known that Fergus wouldn't want to go out, but asking gave Fraser the perfect cover and no one would suspect what he was about to do.

It was time to spy on his brother's future female and make sure she was worthy of a MacKenzie.

Want to read the rest?
The Dragon's Dilemma is available in paperback

For exclusive content and updates, sign up for my newsletter at:

http://www.jessiedonovan.com

Author's Note

I first want to say that while I did a lot of research on preeclampsia and eclampsia complications, any mistakes in the story are my own. I read a lot of firsthand accounts of how the births could go and a few women had been strapped down to the bed like Evie was. The "out of body" experience was also a common reaction to a magnesium sulfate IV drip. Symptoms of preeclampsia can show up much earlier and it is something to watch out for. Always consult a doctor if you think something is off! I just want to make sure all of my readers are safe. :) (I do have a small percentage of male readers. And to you guys, I say watch out for your partner's health!)

Okay, with that out of the way, I have some people to thank:

• Clarissa Yeo is an amazing cover artist and I'm lucky to have her. She captures my dragon-shifters without even really trying.

• Becky Johnson and her team at Hot Tree Editing. Becky always pushes me to be a better writer. Not only that, she gets my humor and writing style. I can't imagine writing without her!

• Iliana, Donna, and Alyson are my awesome beta-readers. Each of them finds different typos and spots out minor problems in the story. They give it the final polish and we all owe them a lot!

And, of course, I thank you, the reader. Not only do you make my dream of writing full-time a reality, you encourage me with comments, feedback, and more. Revisiting characters is extremely time consuming for me as an author, so I really do write these follow-up stories for you. I hope you like them. :)

Thanks again for reading and I can't wait to return to Stonefire for Nikki's story (Sid's story is after hers and then Finn/Ara's follow-up novella). *Surrendering to the Dragon* will be a full-length book and it should be out in May 2016. (Don't worry, there will be another dragon book in February 2016, but that will be for the Lochguard clan!)

Don't forget to sign-up for my newsletter for reveals, sneak peeks, and exclusive contests.

Thanks again for reading and see you around!

ABOUT THE AUTHOR

Jessie Donovan wrote her first story at age five, and after discovering *The Dragonriders of Pern* series by Anne McCaffrey in junior high, she realized people actually wanted to read stories like those floating around inside her head. From there on out, she was determined to tap into her over-active imagination and write a book someday.

After living abroad for five years and earning degrees in Japanese, Anthropology, and Secondary Education, she buckled down and finally wrote her first full-length book. While that story will never see the light of day, it laid the world-building groundwork of what would become her debut paranormal romance, *Blaze of Secrets*. In late 2014 she officially became a *New York Times* and *USA Today* bestselling author.

Jessie loves to interact with readers, and when not reading a book or traipsing around some foreign country on a shoestring, can often be found on Facebook:

http://www.facebook.com/JessieDonovanAuthor

And don't forget to sign-up for her newsletter to receive sneak peeks and inside information. You can sign-up on her website:

http:///www.jessiedonovan.com

24705835R00061

Printed in Great Britain
by Amazon